BENJAMIN
and the Moose

Story by Maureen Spurgeon
Illustrations by Hildrun Covi

Longmeadow Press

Published in North America by Longmeadow Press
201 High Ridge Road, Stamford, CT 05904
English text copyright © 1988 Joshua Morris Publishing, Inc.
Copyright © 1988 Favorit-Verlag
All rights reserved.
Printed in Singapore

The forest was an exciting place for a little brown bear like Benjamin to live.

Every day there was something new and exciting to discover and explore.

Benjamin could watch an eagle nesting among the tall fir trees on the far side of the lake, or see the geese swooping down to the water.

How wonderful it all was!

As Benjamin sat in a tree one day he heard a strange rumbling noise. It was different from the honking of the geese and the chatter of the chipmunks.

Benjamin could not tell where the noise was coming from. Not until he looked down and saw a rather funny-looking animal nibbling away at the bottom of the trunk!

Very soon the tree would come crashing down to the ground!

"Hey!" Benjamin yelled. "Hey, stop gnawing away at my tree!"

But the strange animal just carried on with what he was doing.

"Stop!" Benjamin yelled again, becoming very frightened. "Do you want to send me crashing down, too?"

The little animal suddenly stopped and looked up. Benjamin could see from its large front teeth that it was a beaver.

"Sorry to scare you," Beaver said, "but I need fresh branches and twigs for my home."

Benjamin decided that he had better get down as quickly as possible!

But with each move he made, the tree lurched back further, until Benjamin fell into the lake with a big splash!

Benjamin managed to scramble to the bank. He remembered his father's words about how important it was to keep his ears and eyes open when he was in the forest.

He thought about this until he came to a green meadow.

It was such a beautiful meadow that Benjamin Bear just had to turn lots of somersaults to show how happy he felt!

It was all so peaceful, until a fly decided to rest on Benjamin's nose.

"Get off!" growled Benjamin. He tried to hit the fly with his paw.

But it kept coming back. It tickled Benjamin's nose so much that he gave a great sneeze. And that frightened the fly away!

Just as Benjamin Bear was settling down to take a nap in the meadow, the fly came back.

"I must try to sneeze," Benjamin thought. "That will get rid of it!"

But that was more difficult than he imagined. So Benjamin tried to forget about the fly, until it just flew away.

Suddenly a great, dark shadow loomed over Benjamin. What could it be?

Benjamin could hardly believe his eyes!

A moose was standing right over him! A moose with huge, strong antlers which would frighten even a grizzly bear!

At first Benjamin was very scared. But as the moose looked down at him, Benjamin thought the moose's little black beard made him look very funny.

Benjamin thought he would laugh out loud. But then what would happen, with the moose towering over him as he lay on the ground?

"Little brown bear," said the moose in a kind, gentle voice. "Why are you trembling so? Surely you are not afraid of me?"

Benjamin could not answer he was so scared.

"Moose may be large beasts," the moose went on, "but I certainly did not mean to frighten you. All I wanted was some of the juicy grass in this meadow, same as you. And to think," the moose chuckled, "that my mother used to tell me to keep away from brown bears because they can be quite fierce!"

The thought of the moose being afraid of *him* suddenly made Benjamin burst out laughing. The moose laughed too, rocking his magnificent antlers back and forth.

"Your antlers look like giant shovels!" laughed Benjamin. He was still laughing when the moose scooped him up in his antlers and began marching across the lake.

The animals could hardly believe their eyes, crowding together and watching anxiously to see what would happen next.